The Bat Book

From *The Bat Book & See-Through Model* packaged set, which includes parts for a see-through model bat, and this book.

Bat model and book design by Susan Hernday.

The Bat Book & See-Through Model is produced by becker&mayer!, Ltd.

ISBN: 0-8362-0031-4

Other children's kits by becker&mayer!:

The Amazing Sandcastle Builder's Kit	The American Appaloosa
Build Your Own Dinosaurs	The English Thoroughbred
Fun with Ballet	Fun with Electronics
The Ant Book & See-Through Model	Sleeping Beauty
Build Your Own Bugs	Fun with Electronics, Jr.
Amazing Airplanes Book & Kit	

Special thanks to Elizabeth Stockwell, the University of Washington, and to Catherine Kendall and Scott Smith for their knowledge, support, and clever ideas.

"Bats — strange beings? They fly with their 'hands,' they 'see' with their ears and hang themselves up to sleep by the toes of their hind feet."
— Dr. W. Schober, bat biologist

Bats have been completely misunderstood in our society. People fear bats and have killed them and destroyed their habitat. Yet, without bats thousands of other animals and plants would die—threatening entire ecosystems. Let's learn more about bats, so you can see for yourself how harmless and important they are.

Welcome to the upside-down world of bats, some of the world's most fascinating, beneficial, and likable creatures. Bats live in almost every habitat in the world—all but in the most extreme deserts and at the polar ice caps. They are mammals just like we are, yet they hang upside-down, are nocturnal (hunt at night), and fly.

Ecological Importance of Bats

While you're busy sleeping, bats are greatly benefiting our environment. Insect eaters help farmers and gardeners by controlling populations of crop-destroying insect pests. They can consume thousands of night-flying insects in an evening. Nectar eaters flower-hop, carrying pollen from one bud to the next. To develop fruit, pollen from one flower needs to mix with pollen from another flower. As fruit bats digest fruit, they scatter thousands of seeds in their droppings. They are often the first to reseed a cleared rain forest. Among many others, bats also pollinate banana plants. Could you imagine cereal without bananas?

Most of the world's bats are light enough to be posted as a first-class letter.

Parts of a Bat

As you and bats are both mammals, you may have more in common with them than you think. Mammals are warm to the touch because they are warm-blooded. Most mammals grow inside their mom and are born live. The mothers produce milk for their babies to drink. Mammals have hair or fur as opposed to scales (like reptiles) or feathers (like birds). Bats are the only mammals that have wings and can fly.

The almost one thousand kinds of bats make up a quarter of all mammal species!

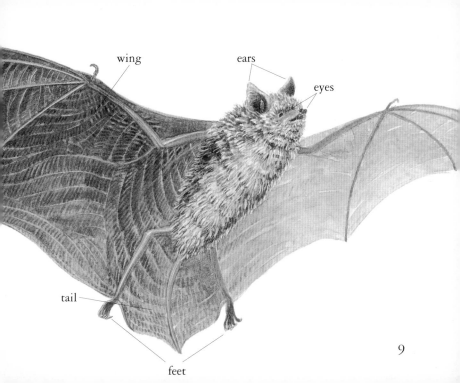

wing

ears

eyes

tail

feet

9

Your Bat Model

Your bat is a common Little Brown Bat whose scientific name is *Myotis lucifugus* (my-OH-tus lu-SIF-ah-gus). Your model is twice as big as a real Little Brown Bat.

Bats are in the group or "order" Chiroptera (ky-ROP-ter-a), which is Greek for "hand-wing." They are divided into Megachiroptera (big bats), which eat fruit and nectar, and Microchiroptera (small bats), which eat mostly insects, but also eat fish, frogs, and fruit. These may sound like big words, but if you can say tyrannosaurus and pterodactyl, bat words should be no problem.

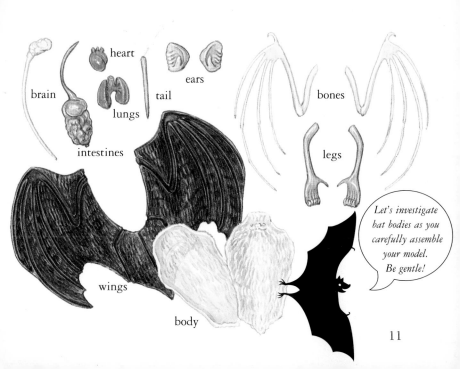

brain

heart

lungs

tail

ears

intestines

bones

legs

wings

body

Let's investigate bat bodies as you carefully assemble your model. Be gentle!

11

The two clear pieces are the body of your bat. All other pieces attach to this body.

Furry Bats

Bat bodies are covered with hair or fur just like other mammals. Hairs insulate and protect the skin. They also serve as both visual and chemical communication. Patterns in the fur are for either camouflage or attraction. Hairs used in chemical communication grow near oil-producing glands on the bats' skin. The oils, which other bats smell, cling to the hairs like paint clings to a paintbrush.

Bats spend more time than teenagers grooming themselves—but bats use their toenails, tongue, and teeth. Healthy bats (and healthy teenagers) keep their parasite population under control.

That boxing glove with a tail is the brain and spinal cord. The brain snaps into the back half of the body.

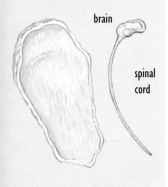

brain

spinal cord

Central Control: The Bat Brain

The spinal cord is the superhighway that carries information between the bat's brain and all the nerves in the body, telling the bat what to do. It is held in place and protected by the *vertebrae* or backbones. The spinal cord in bats is shorter than in other mammals. Since bats don't use their lower body or legs to walk or carry their weight, not as much information needs to go there.

Bats have their own unique personalities, and, like dolphins, are highly intelligent and easily trained.

In megachiroptera, like this Indian Fruit Bat, the front brain, or forebrain, is large. This is the center for vision and smell—important for fruit bats.

In microchiroptera, like this Spotted Bat, the back of the brain, the hindbrain, is larger than the front. This is the hearing and sound center—very important for echolocation.

Snap your bat's digestive system in place.

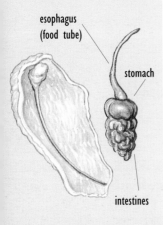

esophagus
(food tube)

stomach

intestines

What Bats Eat

Bats eat fruit, nectar, or insects. Each bat has a stomach suited to digest its favored diet.

Most bats, like your Little Brown Bat, eat insects. Some eat in flight. Others perch to eat large insects and drop the legs, head, and wings in a heap.

Bat caves are often deep with droppings (feces). *Guano* (GWA-no), as bat droppings are called, is harvested and sold as a valuable and nutrient-rich fertilizer.

Bats hang by their thumbs to urinate and drop guano.

Some bats' faces fit the foods they eat. Nectar
eaters have long snouts and tongues. Fruit eaters
have big eyes and doglike snouts. Insectivores have
sensitive ears, the better to hunt in the dark.

Attach the heart to the lungs and place the whole unit in the chest cavity.

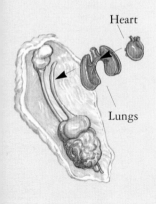

Heart

Lungs

Heart and Lungs—The Inside Scoop

In mammals, bats included, blood gets oxygen from air in the lungs and circulates it and other nutrients through the body in a closed system. Having both a large heart and lungs, bats can pump a lot of oxygen through their blood. Some bat hearts can beat 900–1000 beats per minute (b/m) while in flight. (A human runner's heart may beat 160 b/m.) During hibernation, that same bat heart beats 20 b/m, using a lot less energy.

Bats have a shut-off valve to their wings. This allows them to pump blood through out-stretched wings to cool down or to shut the wing valves and keep the warm blood running only through the trunk of the body.

Like yours, the bat's diaphragm is a muscle that raises and lowers the chest, so the bat can breathe. Fortunately, it isn't gravity that keeps the diaphragm working, or upside-down bats would suffocate.

lungs

diaphragm

liver

heart

stomach

intestines

Bats have all the same internal organs you do. Their heart and lungs are larger than those of other animals their size. Due in part to their difference in diet, insectivores have short intestines, while fruit-eating bats have longer, looping intestines.

19

Carefully snap the front and back of your bat together. Look for the bat's eyes to find its face.

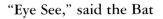

"Eye See," said the Bat

Fruit eaters (megachiroptera) have huge eyes that can see color. Like many nocturnal (active at night) animals, they have a *tapetum lucidum* (TAP-i-tum LOOS-si-dum) which is a special part of the retina that causes the eyes to shine bright red in a spotlight.

Most insect-eating bats use echolocation to navigate and find food. Like your Little Brown Bat, they have small eyes and can only see black and white. Fur can hide their small eyes, which is why people think they're blind. Bats can actually see quite well, even in low-light situations.

Forget "blind as a bat"—bats have great vision.

21

Attach the ears to the head, facing forward.

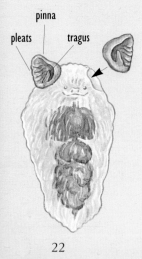

pinna

pleats   tragus

22

Now Ear This

Hearing is the bat's keenest sense. Some bats use a sonar-type signal, called *echolocation* (EK-oh-loh-KAY-shun) to navigate and detect prey (more on page 34). Other bats can hear the slightest sound. African Heart-nosed Bats can hear a beetle's footsteps six feet away.

Megachiroptera (fruit eaters) have small, unexciting ears. Ears of the Microchiroptera come in all shapes and sizes. The big part is the *pinna*. Many *pinnae* are pleated allowing bats to fold their ears.

The *tragus*, like that bump of cartilage inside your ear, serves as an ear shield.

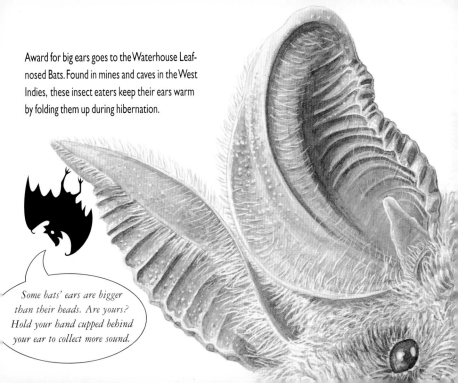

Award for big ears goes to the Waterhouse Leaf-nosed Bats. Found in mines and caves in the West Indies, these insect eaters keep their ears warm by folding them up during hibernation.

Some bats' ears are bigger than their heads. Are yours? Hold your hand cupped behind your ear to collect more sound.

Attach the tail and legs to the body, with toes curling forward.

Bottoms Up

Nearly all bats have some sort of a tail. Like your Little Brown Bat, some have a tail membrane that attaches to their tail. They use this for flight or to scoop up bugs. "Free-tailed" bats have a tail that hangs down longer than the tail membrane.

Look for the *calcar* (KAL-kar), the spur at the ankle that helps support your bat's tail membrane.

Bat knees look like they bend backward because their hip bones are turned out. See how your bat's knees point backward and the bottom of the feet face forward.

Bat toes lock in place so bat can sleep hanging by their feet.

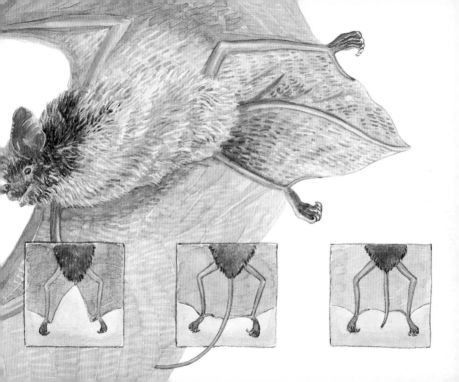

Fit bones into wing grooves and attach the wings to the bat body.

Hands as Wings

Bats fly with their hands! More efficient than a jet, one stroke produces both lift to raise the bat like a kite and thrust to push it forward. The bones in bat wings are the same as your finger bones. The hooked claws are their thumbs. Like your skin, bat wings can heal if punctured. Bats often will wrap their wings around themselves as they hang up for a good day's sleep.

Bats have most of the same bones that you and other mammals have. Their bones are smaller and thinner and, as a result, lighter, but they are not hollow like a bird's bones.

thumb
(first finger)

second
finger

*Bat wings are
as thick as a sandwich
bag and tougher than
a rubber glove.*

fifth finger

third finger

fourth finger

tail

calcar

Putting It All Together

All you need to do now is give your bat a place to rest. First, attach the perch to the bat's feet. Then, you can thread the perch with a string and hang wherever you please! Or, go show off your see-through bat model and tell your friends all about bats.

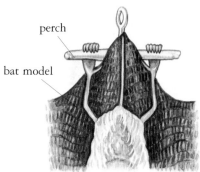

perch

bat model

29

Where Bats Hang Out

The more than one thousand kinds of bats make up a quarter of all mammal species. They live in all but the driest deserts and coldest polar regions. Bats can be found in many places: caves, trees, below bridges, old buildings—some even make tents in palm and banana leaves. When they're not flying, they're hanging upside down.

These beautiful golden Butterfly Bats of southeastern Africa are roosting in small clusters between the leaves of a Natal mahogany tree, about eight feet above the ground.

In the summer, Little Brown Bats live in caves, mines, buildings, tree hollows, and cliff faces. They spend the winter hibernating in humid, frost-free caves or mines.

31

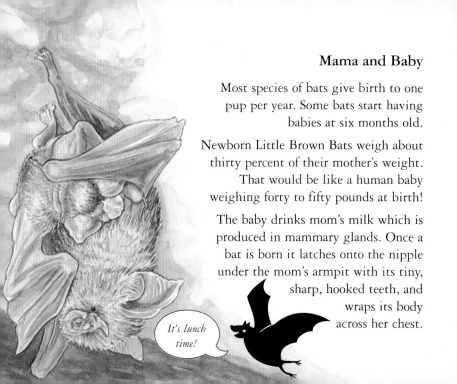

Mama and Baby

Most species of bats give birth to one pup per year. Some bats start having babies at six months old.

Newborn Little Brown Bats weigh about thirty percent of their mother's weight. That would be like a human baby weighing forty to fifty pounds at birth!

The baby drinks mom's milk which is produced in mammary glands. Once a bat is born it latches onto the nipple under the mom's armpit with its tiny, sharp, hooked teeth, and wraps its body across her chest.

It's lunch time!

Hungry baby Horseshoe Bats scream for mom.

Mom goes off for an evening of hunting and returns to a dark cave where thousands of babies cling to the cave walls. There can be hundreds of babies crowded into every square foot. How is she going to find her own? She listens for her baby's special isolation call. Once she finds her baby, she sniffs it, just to be sure.

Bat Chat

Bats can fly around in the dark without crashing into trees or cave walls, and can even detect the thickness of a mosquito antenna! How do they do that? Many bats use echolocation, a built-in sonar system. The bat sends out high-frequency sounds, then listens to the echoes bouncing off things: the mouth of its cave, trees in its way, insects, and other prey. From the echoes, the bat can tell shape, size, texture, how fast something's going, and how far away.

Some bats echolocate with voice or tongue clicks and some send out calls through their nostrils.

When you hear bats squeak and chirp, you're hearing bats "talk" to each other. These sounds are used to show aggression, anger (like when one steals another's food), or other bat communication.

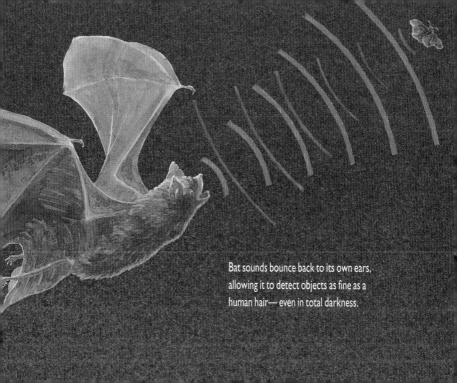

Bat sounds bounce back to its own ears, allowing it to detect objects as fine as a human hair— even in total darkness.

A
*face only a mother
could love.*

Bats Greatest Hits

Bats who send out echolocation calls through their nostrils
have very funny face decorations
called nose-leafs. The proud wearers
of such facial decorations include Slit-
faced Bats, False Vampire Bats, Old and
New World Leaf-nosed Bats, Tube-
Nosed Bats, Horseshoe Bats,
and many more!

Tube-Nosed Bat

Horseshoe Bat

False Vampire Bat

37

Little Brown Bat (*Myotis lucifigus*)

Your bat, the Little Brown Bat, is the most abundant and widespread bat in America. They live in large colonies and often roost in attics, bat houses, and hollow trees. As the longest living small mammal, Little Brown Bats can live up to thirty-two years.

Little Brown Bats weigh only 1/4-ounce, but can eat more than a thousand bugs in a night. The mama bat holds the record. While nursing she needs lots of food and hunts insects four to six hours a night—catching and eating up to six hundred insects an hour. That's about three thousand insects (nearly twice her weight).

Brown Bats hibernate in mines and caves for the winter.

Little Brown Bats digest food in less than an hour—that's fast action!

Vampire Bat *(Desmodus rotundus)*

Not even one percent of all bat species are Vampire Bats. But Vampires sure have given bats a bad reputation.

Vampire Bats live in Latin America and feed mostly on cows, chickens, and other livestock. The bat quietly stalks the chicken and, with its bladelike teeth, bites a 1/5-inch deep hole. A chemical in the bat's spit

keeps the blood
from clotting—
so the blood
flows as the Vampire Bat laps
it up. More than one Vampire
Bat may drink from a single
wound. The animal usually
stays asleep, never knowing it's
been a bat's dinner.

Vampire Bats are blood lickers, not blood suckers!

Flying Fox

Flying Fox bats are the world's largest bat. Their wings stretch out three- to six-feet across and they can weigh up to three pounds. Many live in Asia and Australia. These fruit bats spend the day sleeping in roosting colonies of tall trees in the middle of town. Flying Foxes don't use echolocation, but instead sniff out ripe fruit in the dark, using their sensitive nose and keen eyesight.

Some fruit bats can carry fruit weighing half of their body weight.

Bat Goes Fishing

Using echolocation a Fishing Bat (*Noctilo leporinus*) can detect a fin as fine as a human hair just barely breaking the water's surface. It flies close to the surface, hooks the fish with its

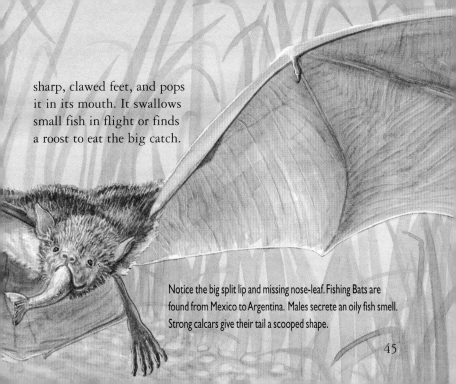

sharp, clawed feet, and pops
it in its mouth. It swallows
small fish in flight or finds
a roost to eat the big catch.

Notice the big split lip and missing nose-leaf. Fishing Bats are
found from Mexico to Argentina. Males secrete an oily fish smell.
Strong calcars give their tail a scooped shape.

45

Nectar Eaters: Lesser Long-nosed Bat

The Lesser Long-nosed Bat (*Leptonycteris curasoae*) makes its nightly meal of nectar from the saguaro, organ-pipe, and cardon cactuses. To feed, the bat does a face-plant, lapping up the nectar with a tongue one-quarter the length of its body. That would be like having a tongue almost as long as your arm!

These bats winter in Mexico and migrate to southwestern United States in the summer. Long-nosed Bats are endangered with only two nursery colonies left in the US.

Bats sometimes take such a pollen bath as they eat that they appear yellow or green.

Tent bats

This Pygmy Fruit Bat
(*Uroderma bilobatum*) makes
a tent by biting the main
ribs of a palm frond, causing
the leaf to droop and fold
around the bat. They are
found in rain forests of
Central and South America.
They have white stripes on
their face and sometimes a
white, skunklike stripe
down their back.

48